Written and Illustrated by

RAYMOND BRIGGS

Jim and the Beanstalk

HAMISH HAM

London

Text and illustrations © Raymond Briggs 1970
First published in Great Britain 1970 by
Hamish Hamilton Ltd
90 Great Russell Street, London, W.C.1
Reprinted 1971
SBN 241 01786 6
Printed in Great Britain by
William Clowes & Sons, Limited
London, Beccles and Colchester

Early one morning Jim woke up and saw an enormous
plant growing outside his window.

"That's funny," he said, "it wasn't there yesterday.
I'll see how high it goes," and he began to climb up
the plant.

"It certainly is a big plant," he said, as he went into the clouds.

When he reached the top of the plant, Jim saw a castle. "I'm hungry," he said. "I'll ask at the castle for breakfast. I hope they have cornflakes."

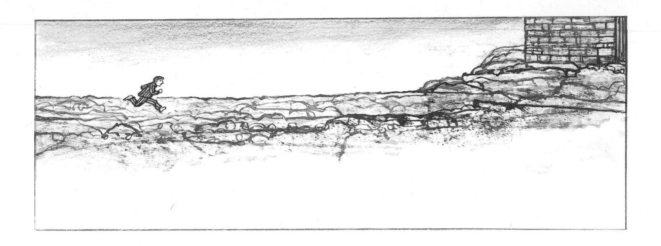

Jim ran to the castle and knocked on the door. He waited and waited, until the door was slowly opened by a very old giant.

"Aha!" said the Giant. "A boy. A nice juicy boy. Three fried boys on a slice of toast – that's what I used to enjoy eating in the old days, but I've got no teeth now. Come in, boy, you're quite safe."

The Giant shared his breakfast of beef and beer with Jim.

"Is your name Jack?" he asked.

"No," said Jim, "it's Jim."

"Did you come up a beanstalk?" asked the Giant.

"I came up some sort of plant," said Jim.

"It's that beanstalk again," said the Giant. "It came up once before. That pesky boy Jack stole some of my father's gold and took our golden harp and our golden hen and I've never really been happy since. And now I'm old, too. I can't even see to read my poetry books because the print is too small."

"Haven't you got any glasses?" asked Jim.

"Only beer glasses," said the Giant.

"I mean reading glasses," said Jim. "They go on your nose and ears."

"It's my eyes I'm talking about!" roared the Giant, banging his fist on the table.

"These glasses are *for* your eyes," said Jim, and he explained about glasses while the Giant listened carefully. "Get 'em!" said the Giant fiercely when Jim had finished. "Get 'em for me. I'll pay good gold."

"I'll have to measure you," said Jim.
So Jim measured the Giant's head.

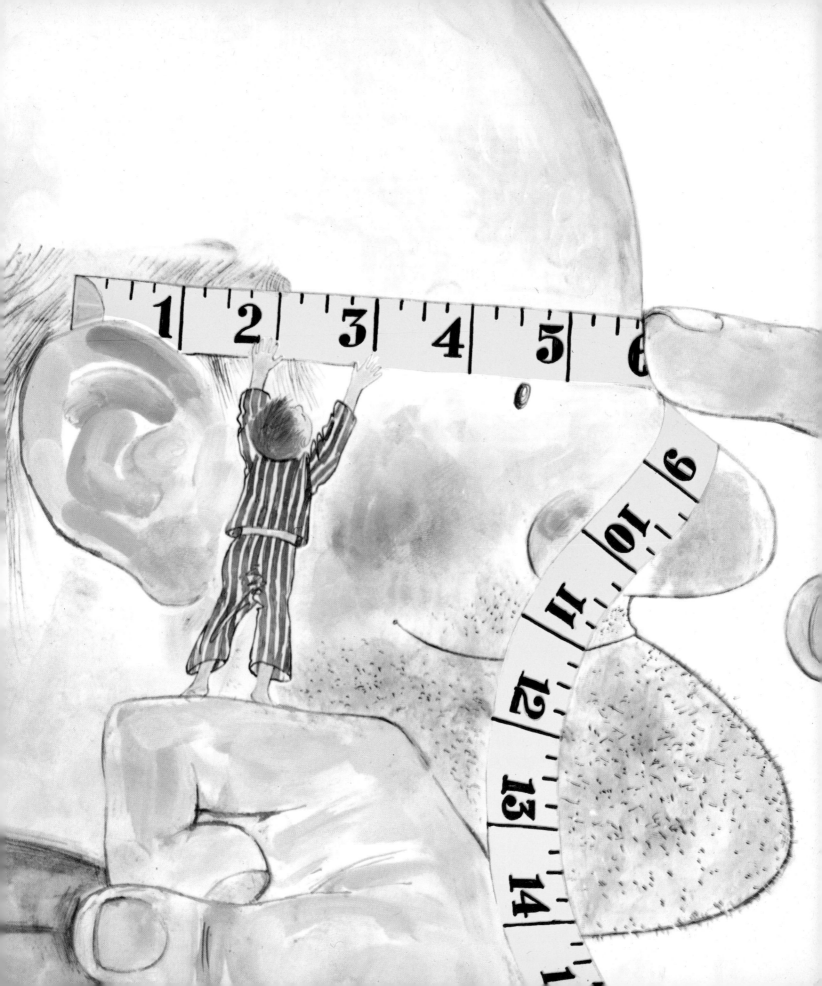

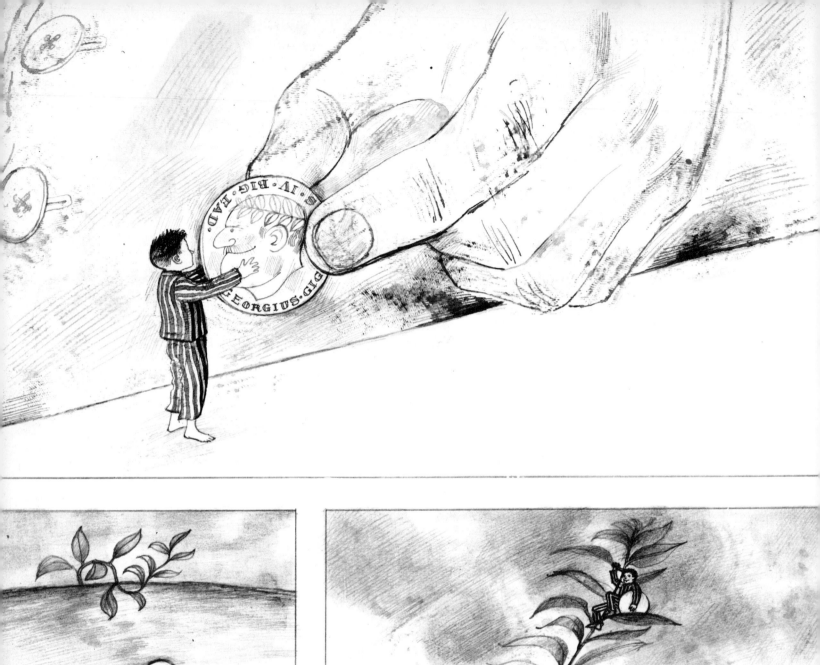

The Giant gave Jim a gold coin, and Jim climbed down the
beanstalk as fast as he could, holding tight to the coin.
He showed the coin to his mother, but before she could say
anything he got dressed and ran off to the oculist.

The oculist could hardly believe his eyes when he saw the giant gold coin, but he set to work straight away. He worked all night, and in the morning the glasses were ready.

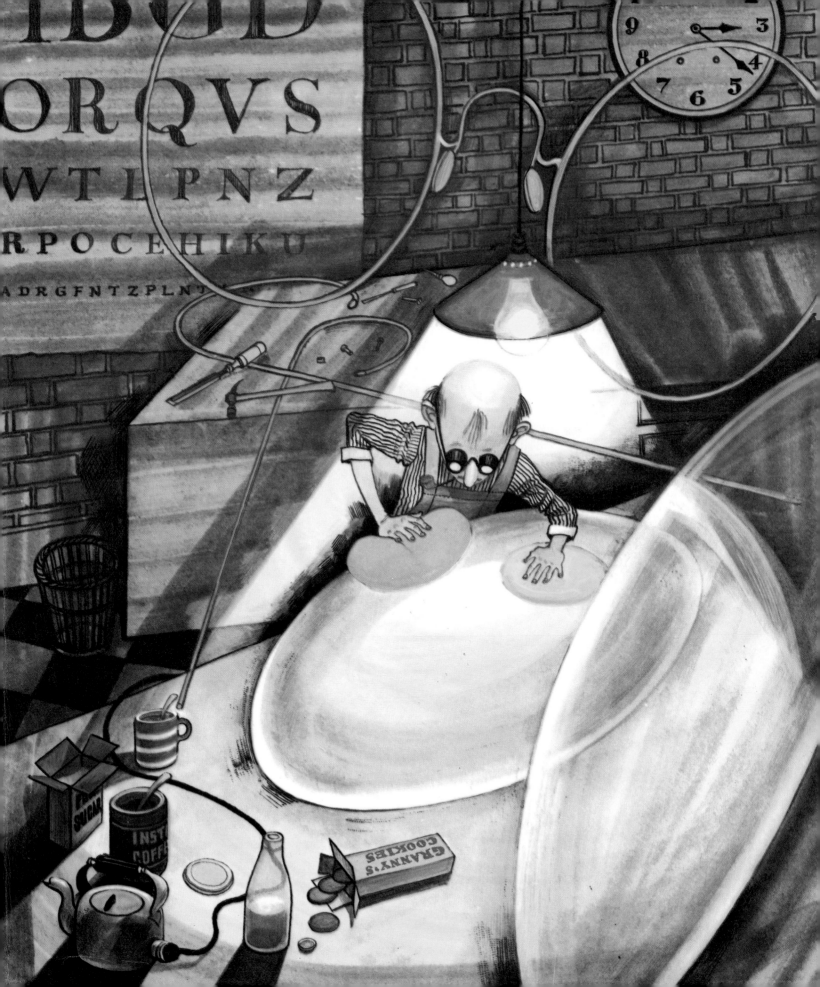

Jim carried them home. Then he tied them on his back and climbed up the beanstalk.

The Giant loved his glasses and began reading rhymes to Jim as soon as he put them on.

"You're a good boy," he said. "Now I can see you properly I wonder what you'd be like to eat? I can't eat anything much nowadays because I've got no teeth."

"Why don't you have false teeth?" asked Jim.

"False teeth!" roared the Giant. "Never heard of them!"

So Jim explained about false teeth while the Giant listened carefully.

"Get 'em!" said the Giant when Jim had finished. "Get 'em for me. I'll pay good gold."

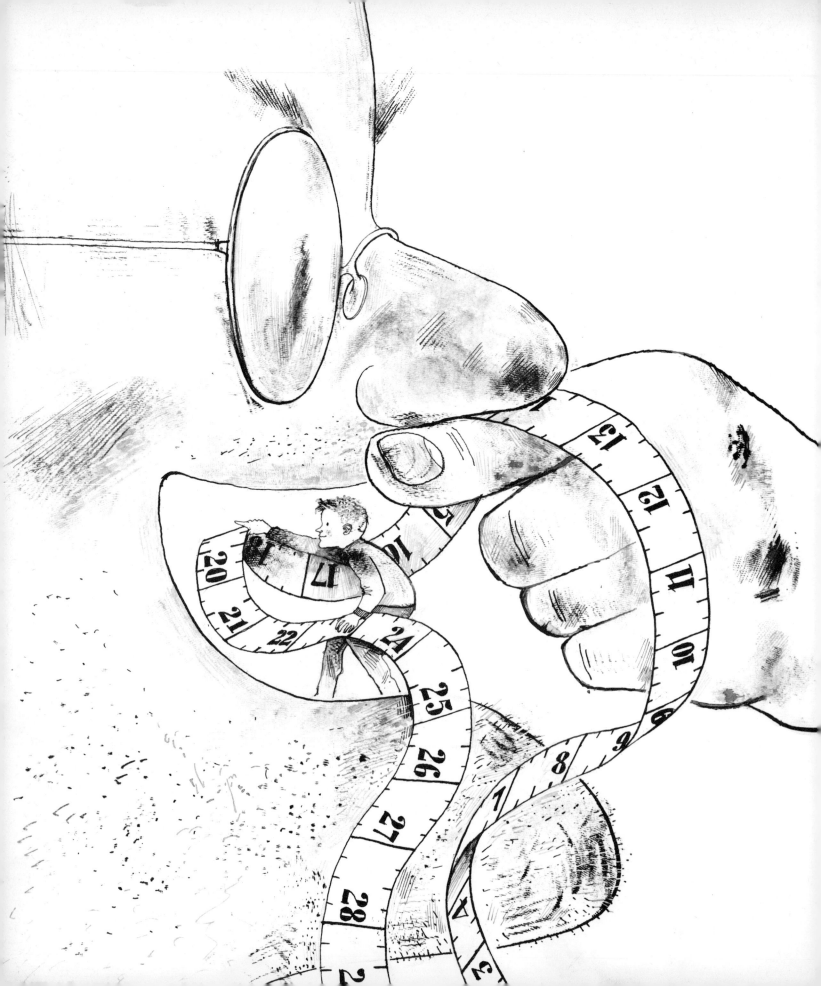

So Jim measured the Giant's mouth. "Make them big,"
said the Giant, "and sharp. I like sharp teeth."

The Giant gave Jim another gold coin and Jim climbed
down the beanstalk as fast as he could, holding tight to
the coin. He showed the coin to his mother, but before she
could say anything he ran off to the dentist.

The dentist could hardly believe his eyes when he saw the giant gold coin, but he set to work straight away. He worked all night, and in the morning the teeth were ready.

Jim carried them home. Then he tied them on his back and climbed up the beanstalk.

The Giant loved his new teeth. He jumped up and down, champing his jaws and gnashing the teeth until the sparks flew.

Then the Giant sat down and looked at himself in a mirror.

"Ah," he said, "I used to be a good-looking lad. Great head of flaming red hair I had, and now look at me."

"Why don't you have a wig?" asked Jim.

"A wig!" roared the Giant. "Never heard of a wig!"

So Jim explained about wigs while the Giant listened carefully.

"Get one!" said the Giant when Jim had finished. "Get one that's red and curly! I'll pay good gold."

So Jim measured the rest of the Giant's head.

The Giant gave Jim another gold coin, and Jim climbed down the beanstalk as fast as he could, holding tight to the coin. He showed the coin to his mother, but before she could say anything he ran off to the wig-maker.

The wig-maker could hardly believe his eyes when he saw the giant gold coin, but he set to work straight away. He worked all night, and in the morning the wig was ready.

Jim carried it home. Then he tied it on his back and climbed up the beanstalk.

The Giant loved his wig. "I look about a hundred years younger!" he said.

He put on all his best clothes and danced about the room, beaming at himself in the mirror.

"Marvellous! Wonderful!" he boomed. "I'm happy again. I feel like a new Giant. And my appetite has come back, too. . . ."